# DC™ SUPER-PETS!

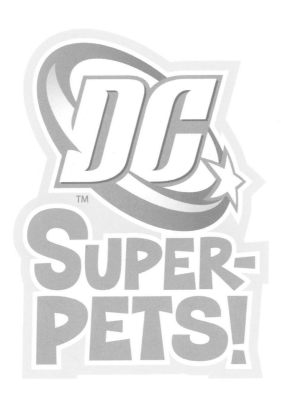

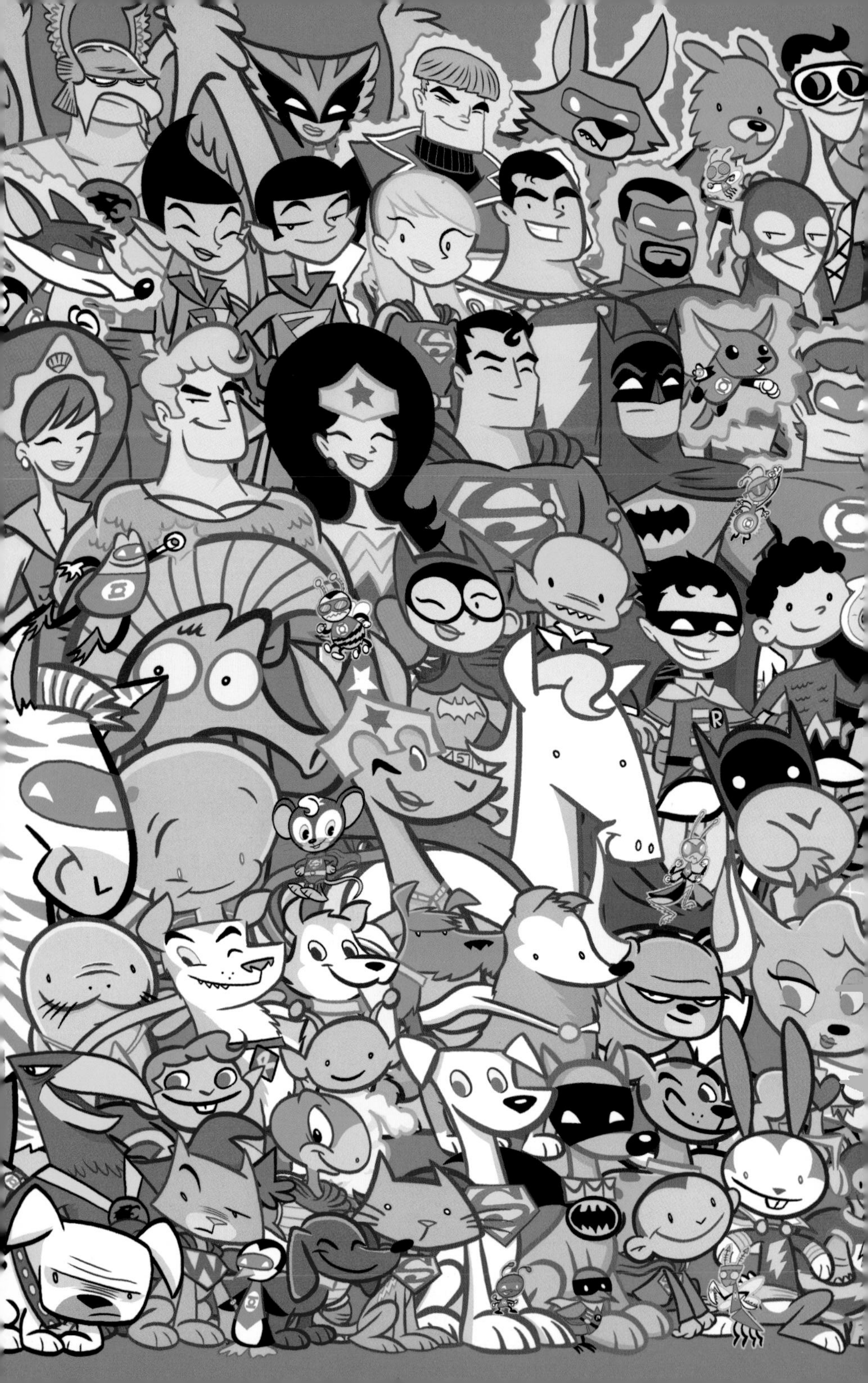

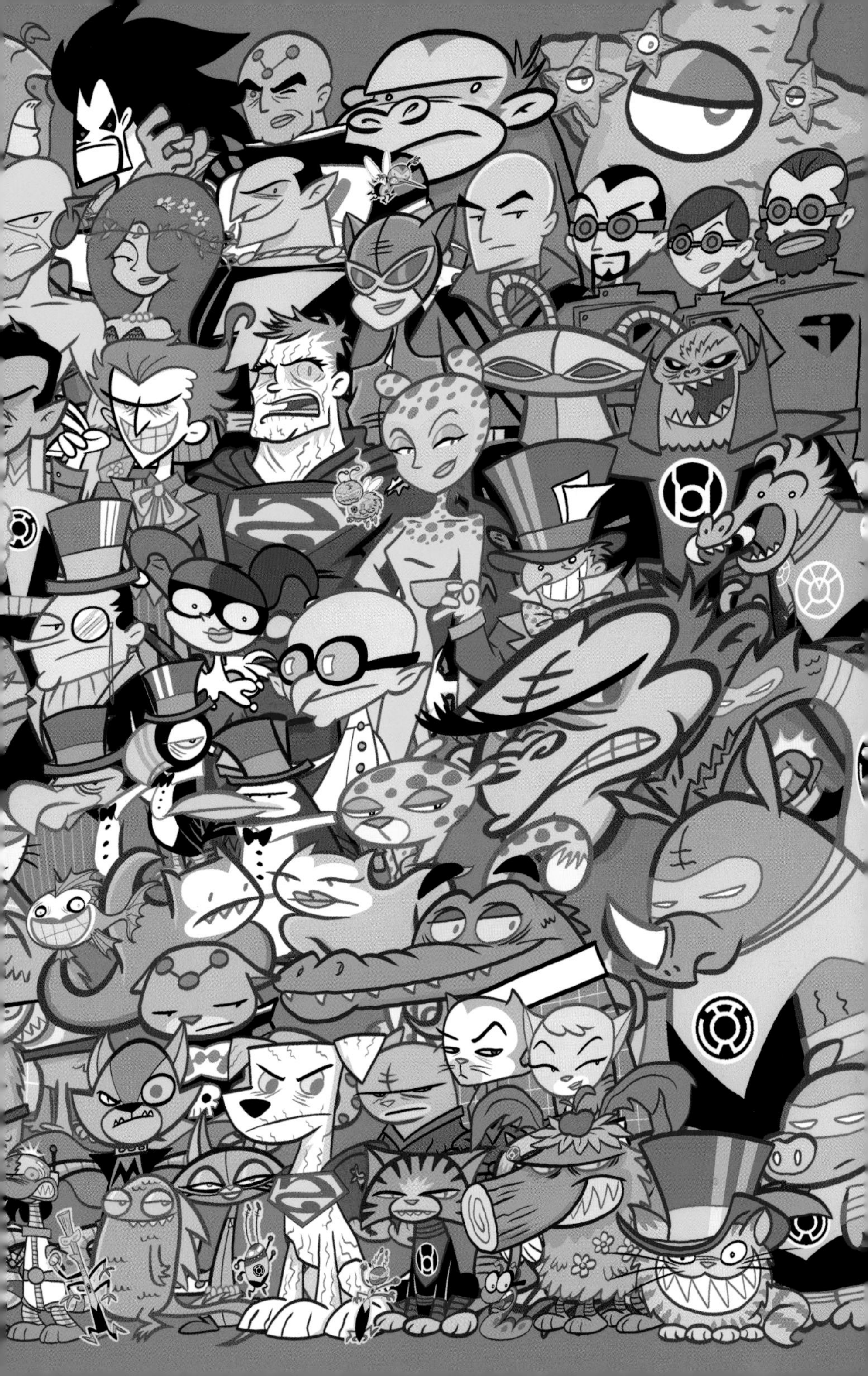

DC™
SUPER-PETS!

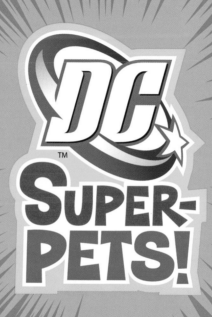

# STARRO AND THE SPACE DOLPHINS

by
Art Baltazar

Lobo created by Roger Slifer and Keith Giffen
Hawkman created by Gardner Fox

PICTURE WINDOW BOOKS™
a capstone imprint

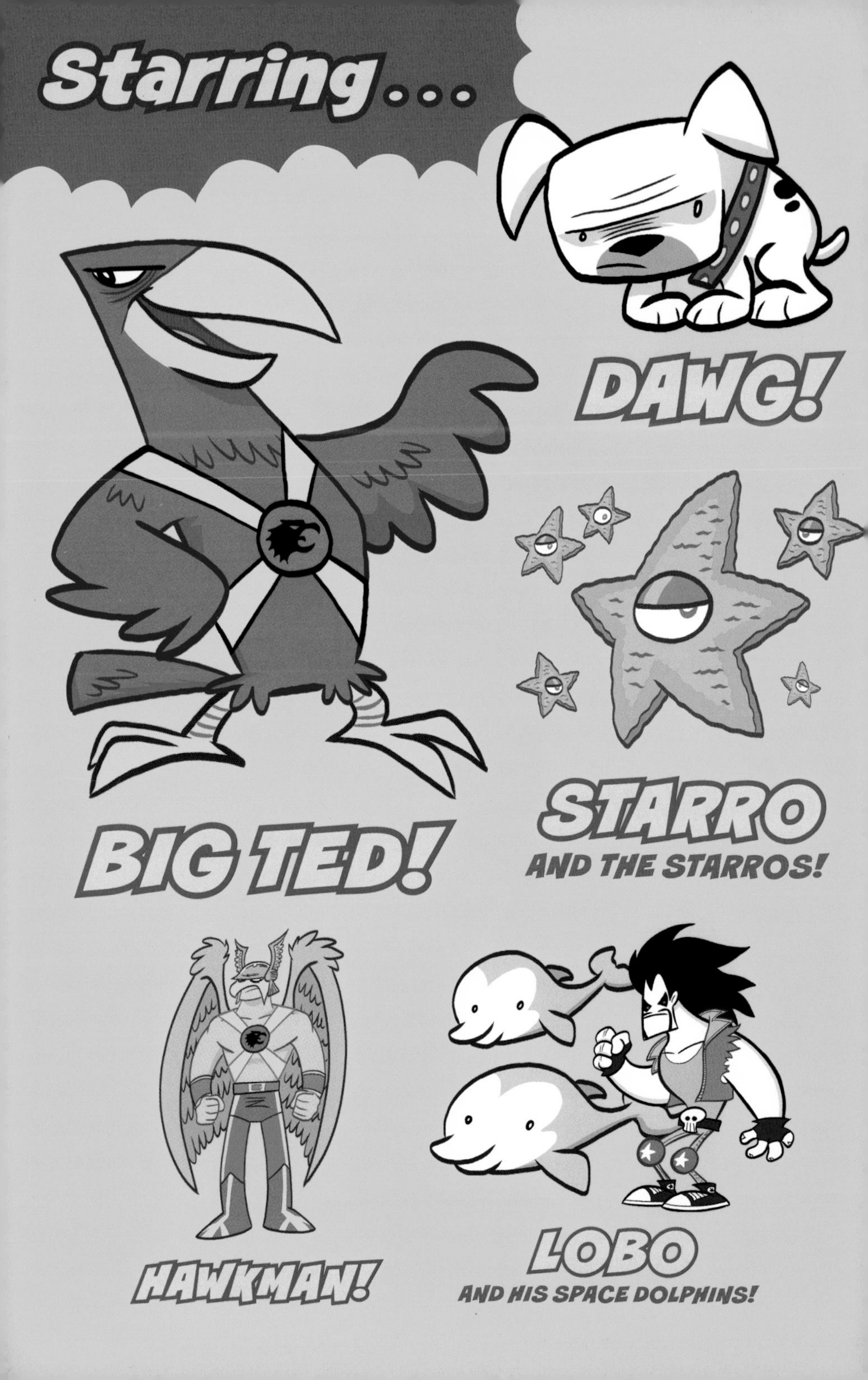
Starring...
DAWG!
BIG TED!
STARRO
AND THE STARROS!
HAWKMAN!
LOBO
AND HIS SPACE DOLPHINS!

# TABLE OF CONTENTS!

**Meet Big Ted!** 4

Chapter 1
## TO THE RESCUE! 6

Chapter 2
## STOLEN DOLPHINS 15

Chapter 3
## STARRO! 26

**More fun!** 50-56

## SUPER-PET HERO FILE 017:
# BIG TED

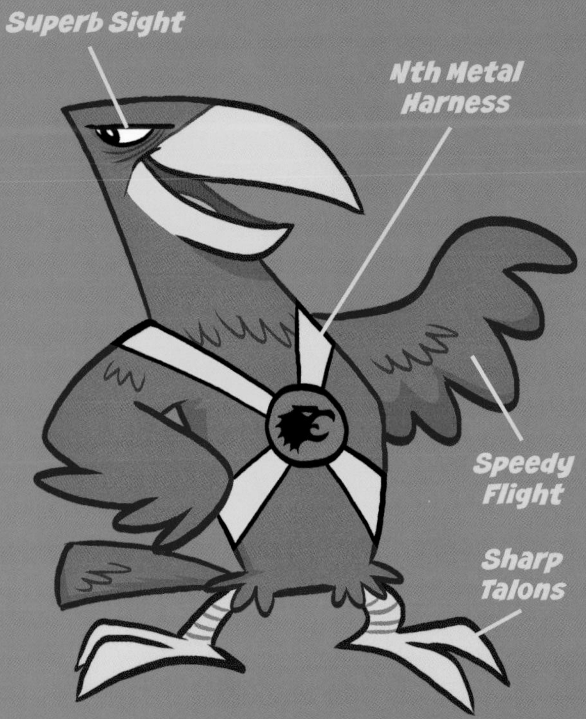
Superb Sight
Nth Metal Harness
Speedy Flight
Sharp Talons

**Super Hero Owners:**

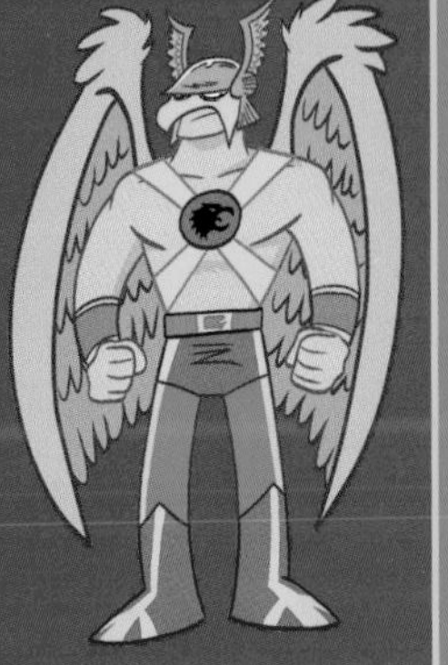

HAWKMAN

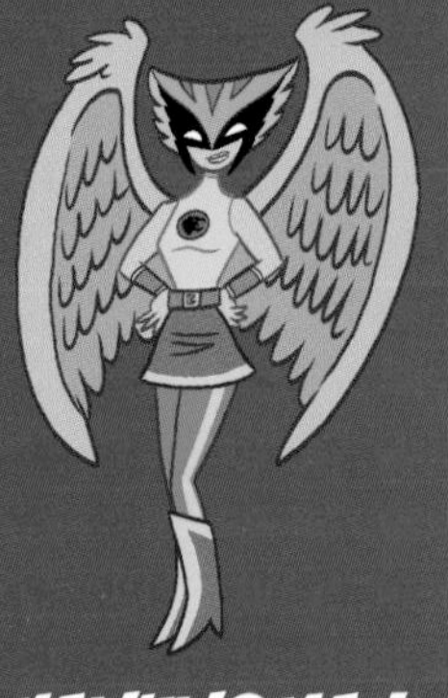

HAWKWOMAN

**Species:** Red Hawk
**Place of Birth:** Hawk Valley
**Age:** Unknown
**Favorite Food:** Hoagies

**Bio:** Since hatching from an egg, Big Ted has helped his high-flying owners catch their prey.

# SUPER-PET HERO FILE 018:
# DAWG

Thick Skull

Tracking Skills

Scrappy

Super Hero Owner:
**LOBO**

## Super-Pet Enemy File 017:
## STARROS

Cloning Powers

Mind Control

Freaky Eyes

Super-villain Owner:
**STARRO**

# Chapter 1

# TO THE RESCUE!

## SWOOOOOSH!

"Let's go, **Big Ted!**" shouted

**Hawkman** as his spaceship zoomed

through deep space. "That alien

spacecraft is spinning out of control.

It's on a collision course with the sun!"

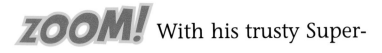 With his trusty Super-Pet beside him, Hawkman piloted his ship through outer space. The heroes quickly caught up to the troubled craft.

**"Launch the Anti-gravity Beam!"**

Hawkman shouted.

**"Roger that!"** replied Big Ted.

With the flip of a switch, Hawkman's ship fired a bright beam.

**BWEEOOM!** The beam caught the alien spacecraft and brought it to a crawl. Finally, the aliens were safe.

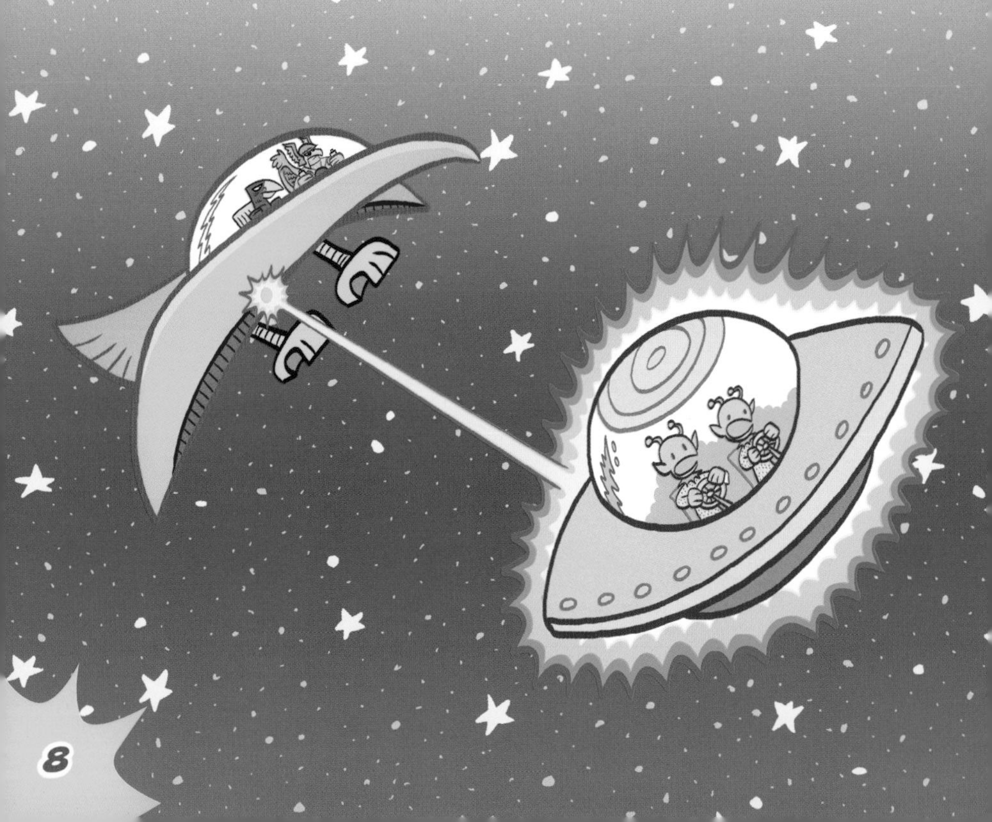

"Check the monitors, Big Ted," ordered Hawkman. "Make sure our alien friends are all right."

**CLICK!** With a press of another button, Big Ted activated a monitor to look inside the alien spacecraft.

"Thank you for saving us!" the aliens cheered. "A giant starfish monster spun us out of control. We didn't know what to do!"

**"Starfish monster?"** Hawkman wondered aloud. **"Very interesting."**

At that moment, another alarm started blaring in the ship.

 **"Hawkman!"** shouted Big Ted. **"Someone else is in trouble, and it sounds like . . . crying."**

"Yes, that sounds like a cry for help," said Hawkman. "Let's go, Big Ted!"

Hawkman and Big Ted strapped on their safety belts. The winged super hero gripped the steering wheel while his Super-Pet pressed a big red button.

**SWOOOOOSH!**

The ship's engines fired up, and the Hawk heroes blasted off through the stars!

Soon, the ship arrived in a dark, empty area of deep space. The alarm kept ringing, but the source of the signal was nowhere in sight.

"I don't see anything, Hawkman," said Big Ted. "Just lots of nothing."

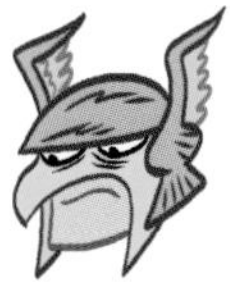

**"Yes, this is very strange,"** answered Hawkman. **"The distress call led us to — Wait! Look over there!"**

Hawkman pointed out the window of the ship. "What's that floating in space?" he asked his Super-Pet partner. **"Is that a . . . motorcycle?"**

Hawkman and Big Ted stared out of the cockpit. Nearby, a lone space-bike floated among the stars.

The biker was a large, pale, scruffy man. He had a mustache and long, bushy hair. His muscles bulged through his vest that had once been a jacket. The stranger's red eyes recognized the heroes.

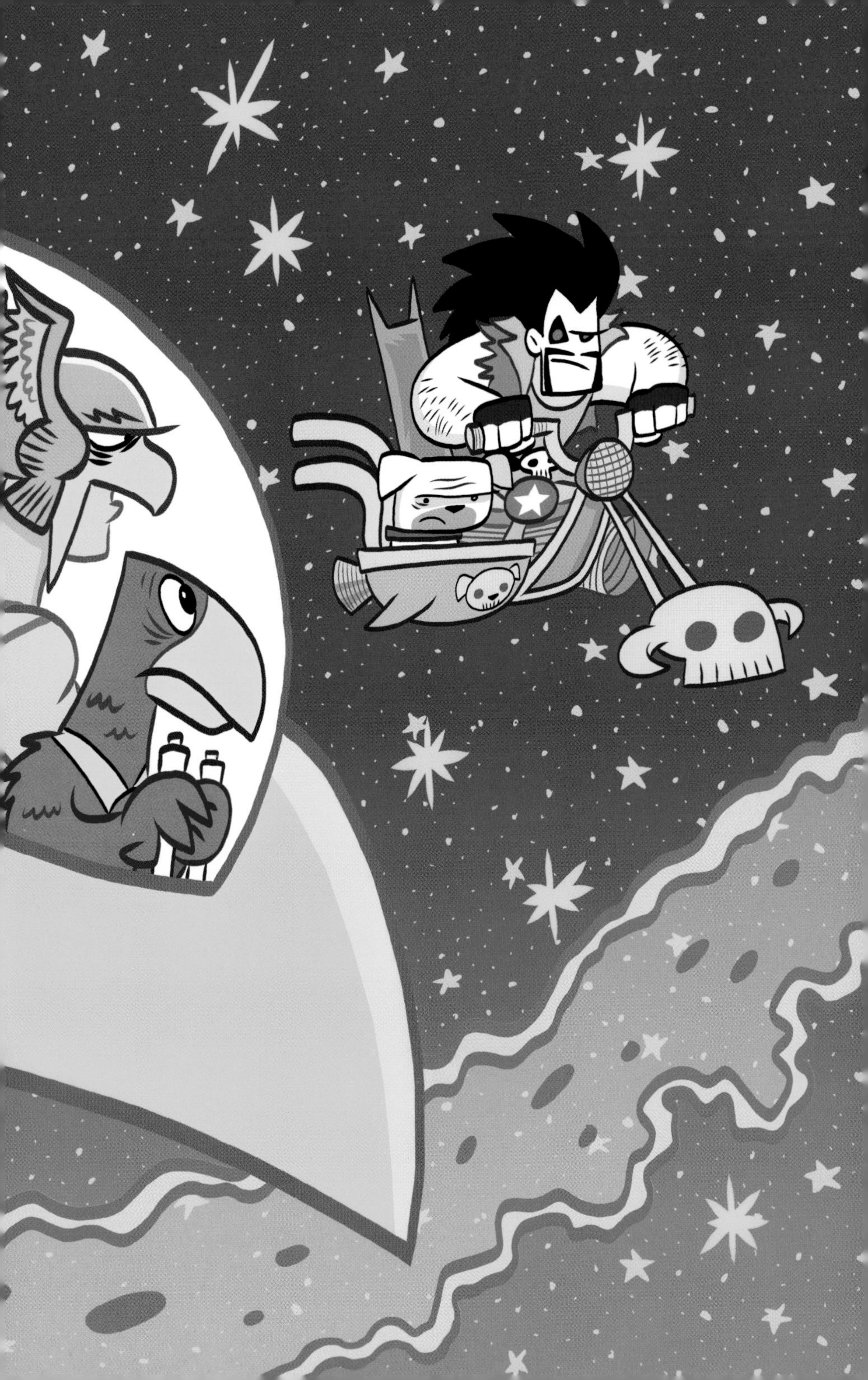

"Hey there," said the biker in a deep voice. "Thank you for answering my call. My name is **Lobo,** and this is my pet dog, **Dawg.**" Lobo pointed at the motorcycle's sidecar. His bulldog sat inside, panting and slobbering.

"I'm glad you're here," Lobo added. "Someone has stolen my Space Dolphins . . . **and they've got to pay!**"

# Chapter 2

# STOLEN DOLPHINS

Hawkman couldn't believe his ears. He stepped out of his spaceship and flew closer to the stranger. "Did you say dolphins?" he asked.

"That's right," Lobo replied. **"Space Dolphins!"**

"Okay, let me explain," Lobo continued. "You see, the Space Dolphins are the most intelligent and beautiful creatures in all of deep space. They're very nice and a real pleasure to hang out with. I sure like the way they dance, too. They are a wonderful sight to see!"

**Dawg cried from the sidecar.**

"It sounds like Dawg really misses them, too," Big Ted said from the ship.

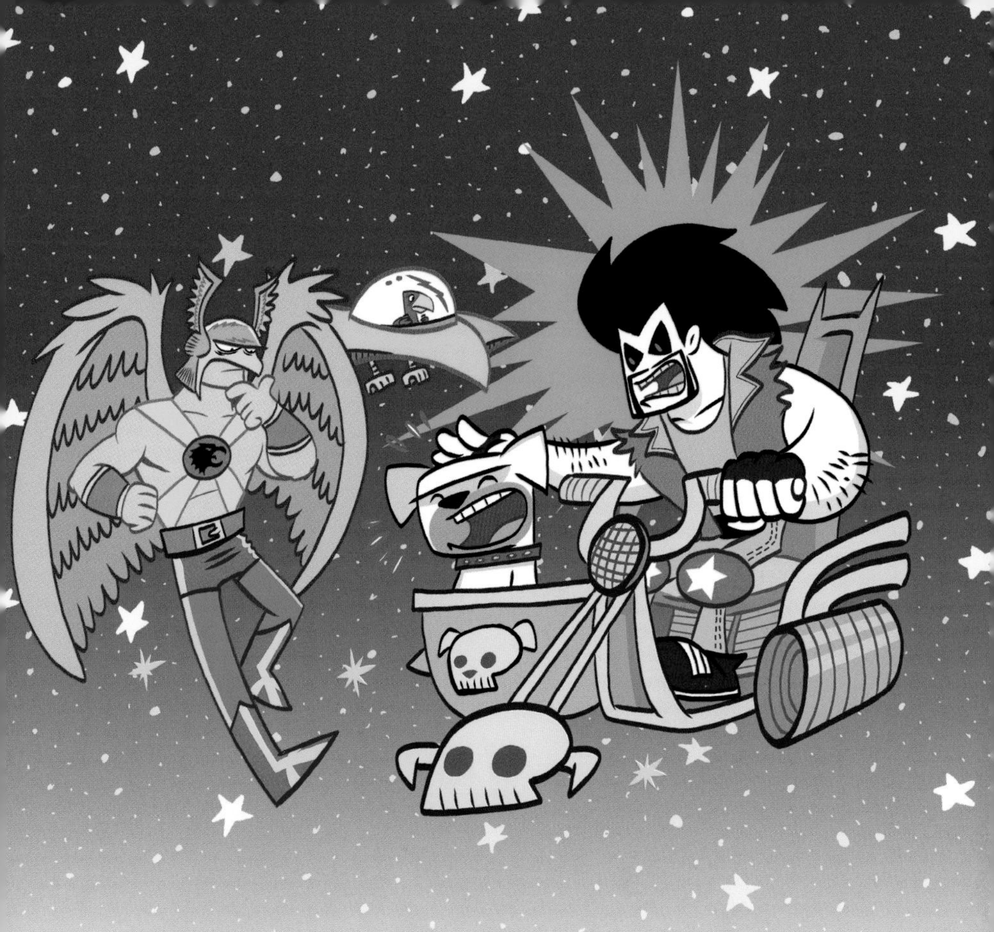

**"Yep, they were his favorite friends,"** replied Lobo, patting his poor pup.

"So where should we start looking for these Space Dolphins?" asked Hawkman. "Who could have taken them, Lobo?"

The space biker reached into a sack with his thick finger and thumb. He pulled out a **small purple starfish.**

"Maybe we could ask HIM!" Lobo said, shaking the one-eyed creature.

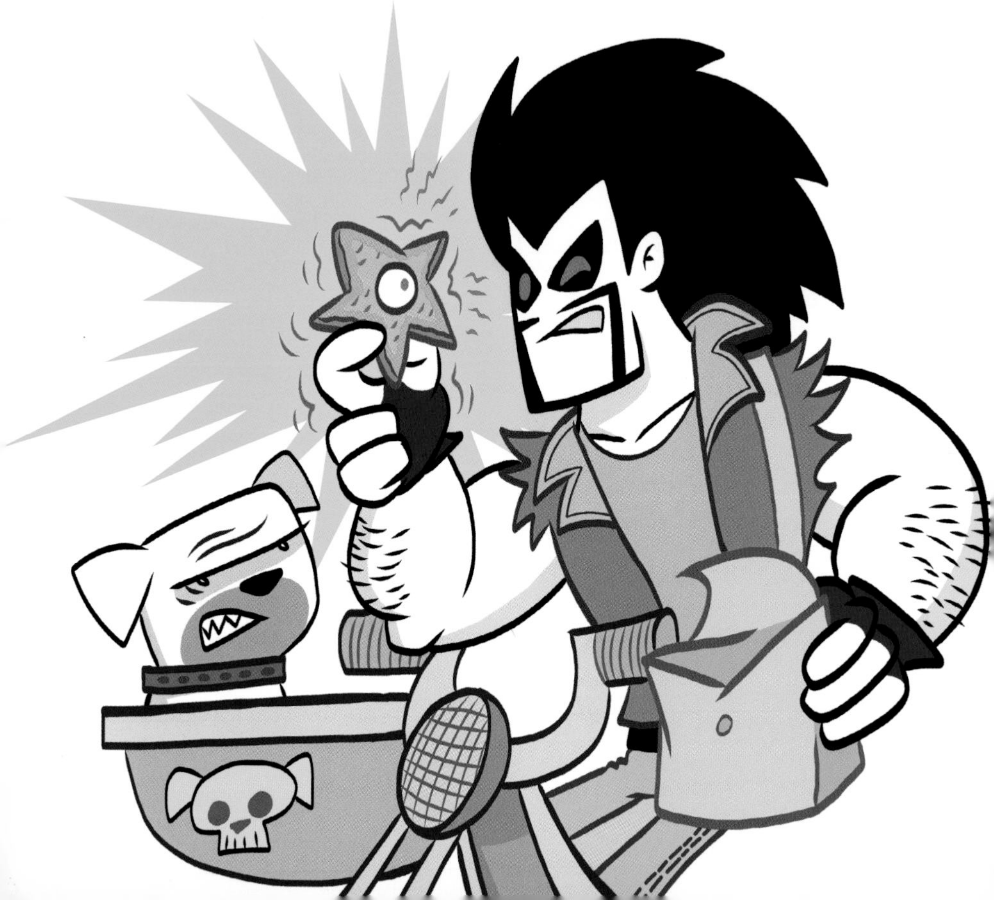

Lobo stared into the little starfish's eye. **"Where are my Dolphins, you** 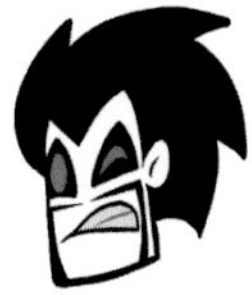 **five-pointed fool?"** he asked, angrily.

**"Beware the Starro!"** the starfish muttered through Lobo's grip. "He will get you!"

"Why you little —!" Lobo shouted. He gripped the starfish tighter, nearly squishing the creature in his palm. "I'll turn you into starfish sushi!"

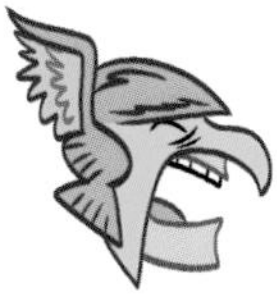

**"No, wait!"** Hawkman cried out. **"Don't hurt him!"**

Lobo loosened his grip on the evil starfish and looked up at Hawkman.

"Why not?" Lobo asked, puzzled. "This one-eyed nitwit knows who took my Space Dolphins."

"Exactly," said Hawkman. "These space starfish are mind-controlling aliens. I bet this one can lead us back to its master."

"Great idea, Hawkman!" said Lobo. "Why didn't I think of this sooner?"

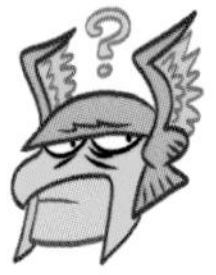

**"Of what?"** wondered Hawkman.

Before Lobo could answer, he slapped the starfish onto his face. With the starfish attached, Lobo's brain became one with the evil creature. Its mind control powers would lead the heroes straight to the Space Dolphins and the leader of the Starfish Gang.

Suddenly, Lobo's space-bike started up and began to shake.

**VROOM! VROOM!**

The motorcycle took off. Lobo streaked through space, leaving a cloud of space dust and his pet dog, Dawg, in the sidecar behind.

**ZOOOOOOOMM!**

"Wait!!" shouted Hawkman, but Lobo was already gone. The winged hero turned to Dawg. "That creature is totally controlling Lobo!"

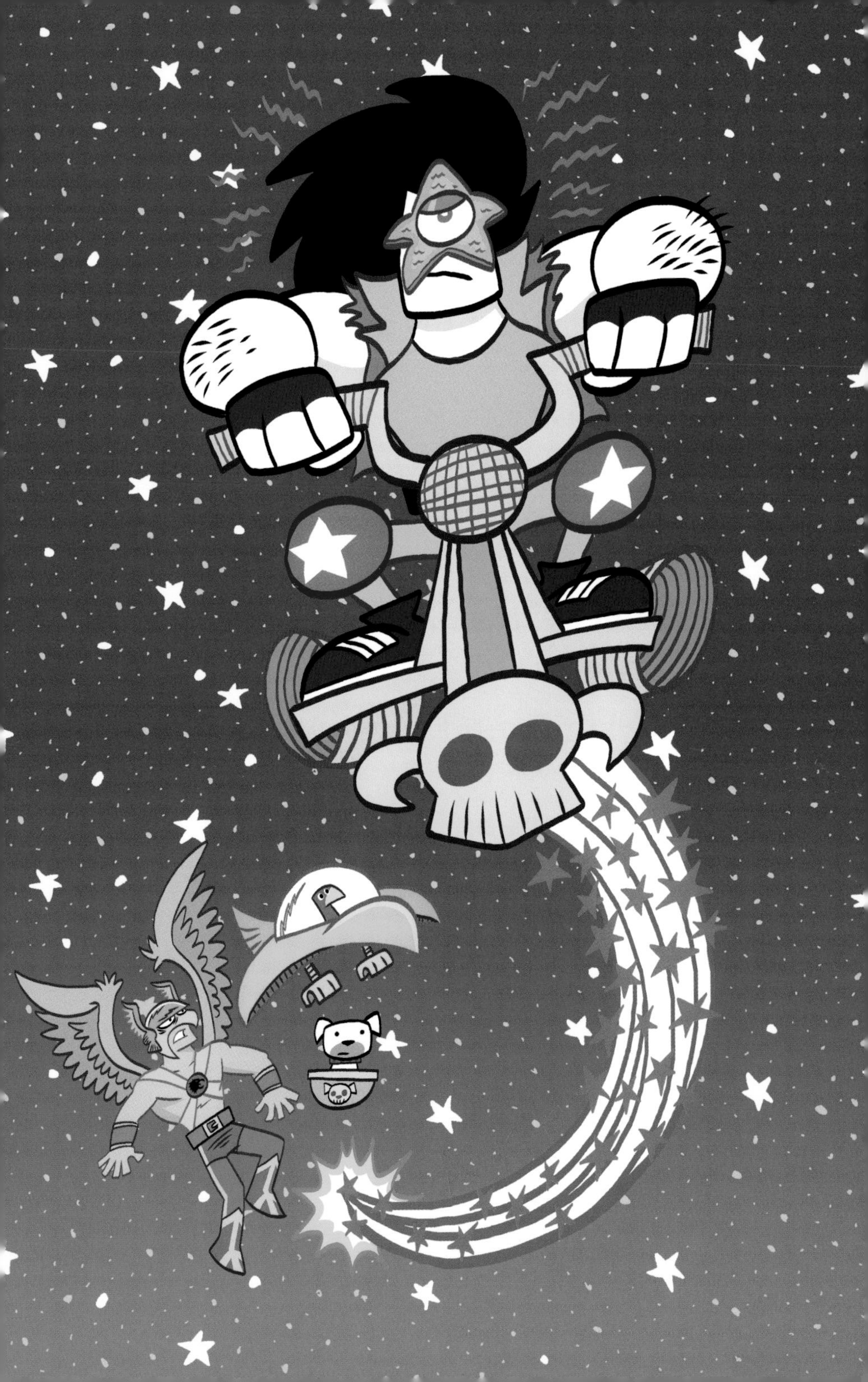

"If we follow him," Hawkman continued, "he should lead us to the Space Dolphins and maybe the mysterious Starro!"

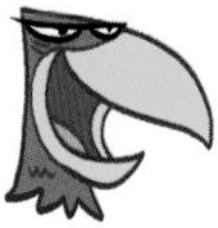

**"Right, Hawkman!"** Big Ted confirmed. **"What are we waiting for?"**

Hawkman and Dawg hopped into the spaceship as Big Ted prepared for full speed ahead.

"Follow the trail of space dust, Big Ted!" Hawkman shouted. "We can't let them get away!"

"Right again, Hawkman!" answered his trusty Super-Pet.

FWOOSH! The ship zoomed through outer space in pursuit of the mind-controlling starfish and the speeding space-bike.

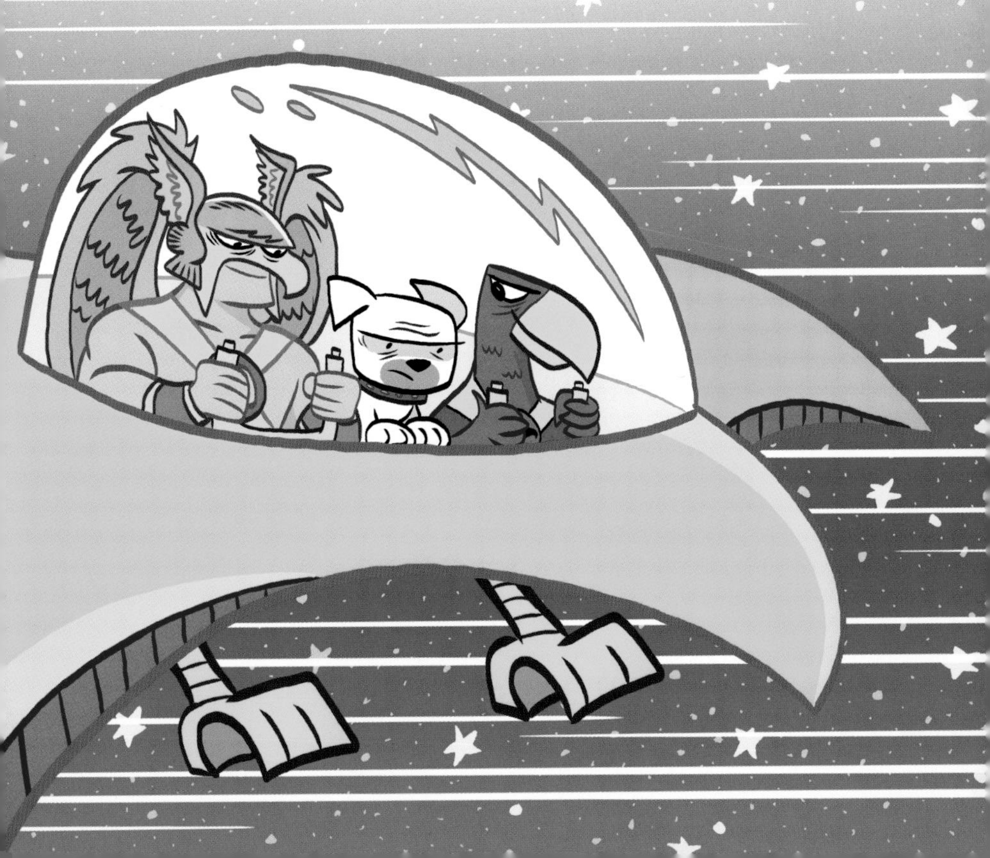

# Chapter 3

# STARRO!

**"Increase speed, Big Ted!"**

ordered Hawkman. The ship continued

following the speeding space-bike. "We

are losing sight of Lobo!"

"Look, Hawkman!" said Big Ted.

"The evil starfish is leading Lobo right

to that small, crusty moon!"

"That's no ordinary moon," warned Hawkman. "That's the nastiest moon of all. It's known across the galaxy as the **Evil Starro Moon!** We must be careful. There's no telling what sinister surprises may be waiting for us!"

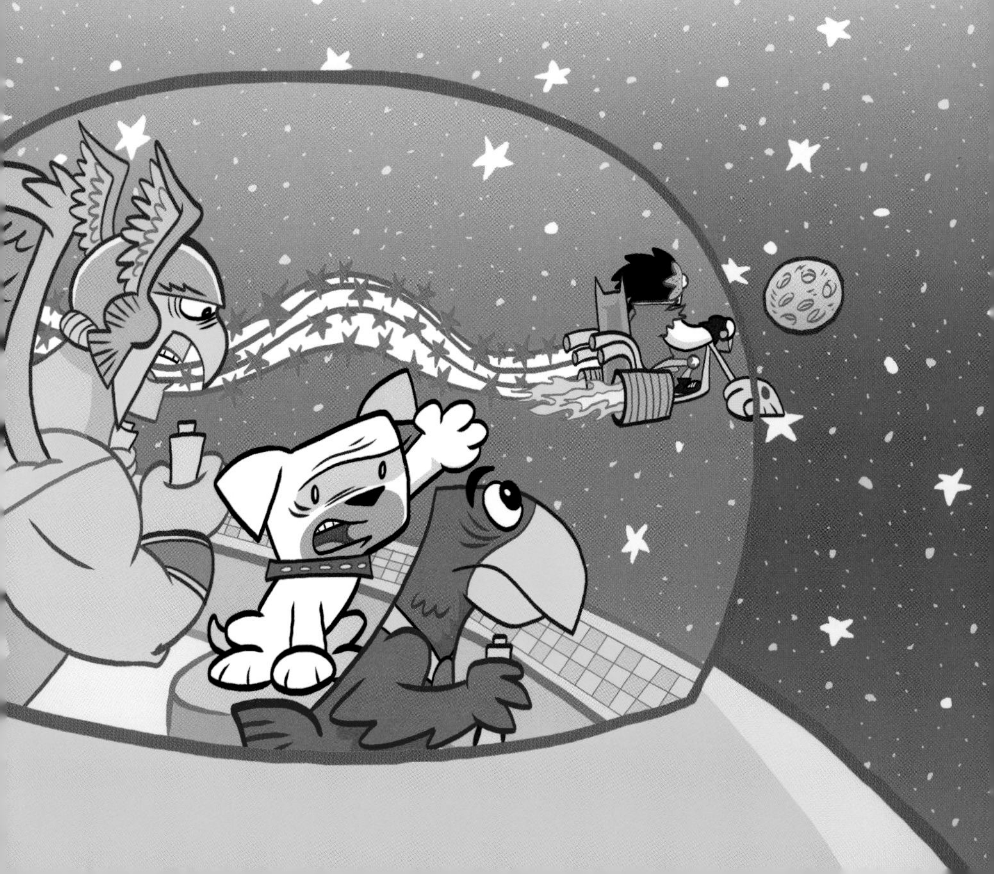

 **"Gulp!"** Big Ted and his new friend Dawg swallowed with fear.

Lobo's space-bike swooped down into a moon crater and out of sight. As soon as his bike disappeared, hundreds of one-eyed Starros rose from the crater like a swarm of bats.

# FWIP! FWIP! FWIP!

They surrounded Hawkman's ship!

"We're under attack!" shouted Big Ted. "I can't see! We must make an emergency landing."

As soon as the heroes were safely on the ground, the evil Starros began tearing at the ship.

"They're ripping the ship apart!" yelled Hawkman. "Cover your faces!"

Big Ted and Dawg listened to Hawkman's words. Their feathers and paws covered each other's faces. The Starros swirled every which way around them.

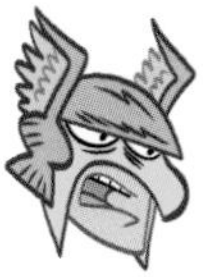

**"They can't control you if they can't land on your face!"** said Hawkman.

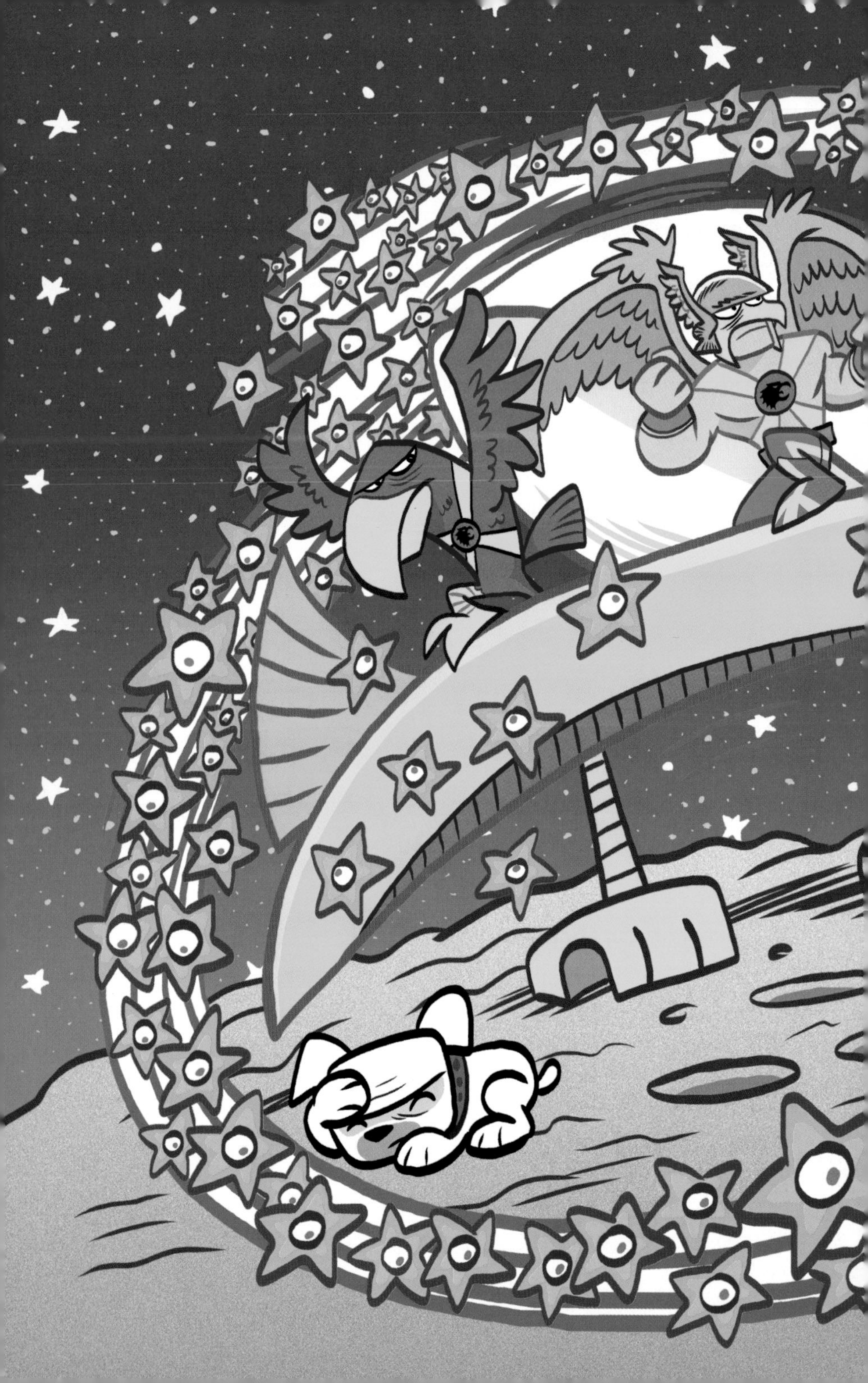

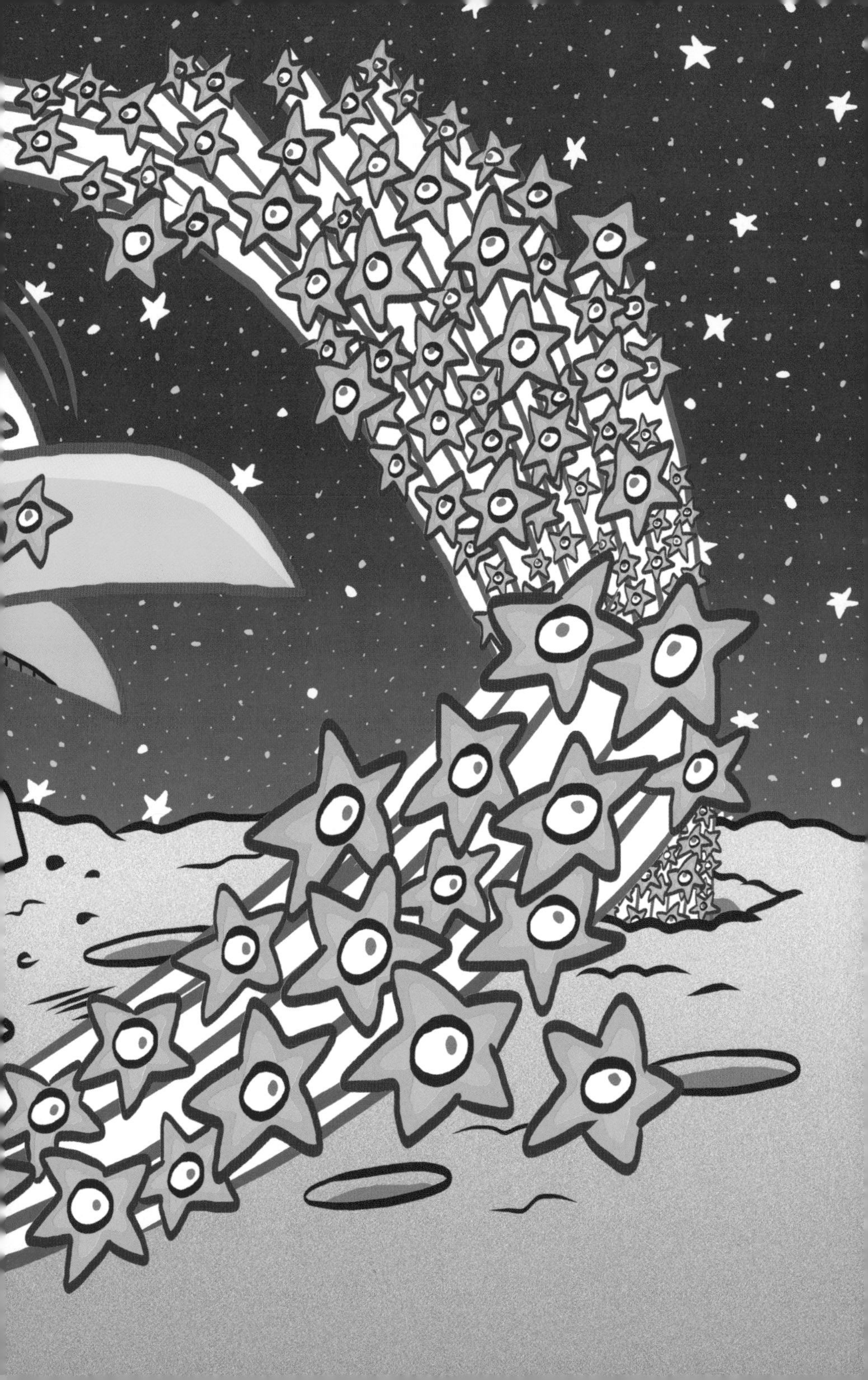

After a few seconds, the Super-Pets uncovered their faces. They were shocked to see . . . nothing! The Starros and Hawkman were gone.

"Oh no! Hawkman's been taken by the evil Starros," cried Big Ted. "They must have gone into the crater. It's time for the Super-Pets to band together and save our hero partners!"

 **WOOF! Dawg agreed.**

Big Ted lifted Dawg by the collar. Together, they flew into the dark crater.

"Sure is scary down here!" Big Ted said as he zoomed deeper and deeper into the crater. "I can't see a thing!"

Suddenly, the Super-Pets heard a faint sound of music coming from within the crater.

Then a voice echoed from the cave, "A one . . . a two . . . a three . . ."

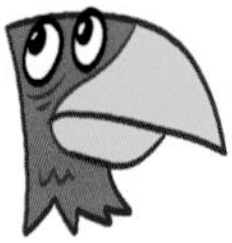

**"Did you hear that, Dawg? It sounds like there is some kind of concert going on in here,"** said Big Ted. **"Let's investigate!"**

Big Ted and Dawg carefully snuck their way in the direction of the music. As they reached the end of the cavern, the Super-Pets peered over a ledge and spotted a large concert hall.

A **giant Starro** floated on the stage!

The evil alien was holding a

conductor's baton and directing a

concert of Space Dolphins. Each one

had a mind-controlling Starro stuck

to its face. Hawkman and Lobo were

playing musical instruments with

Starros on their faces, too!

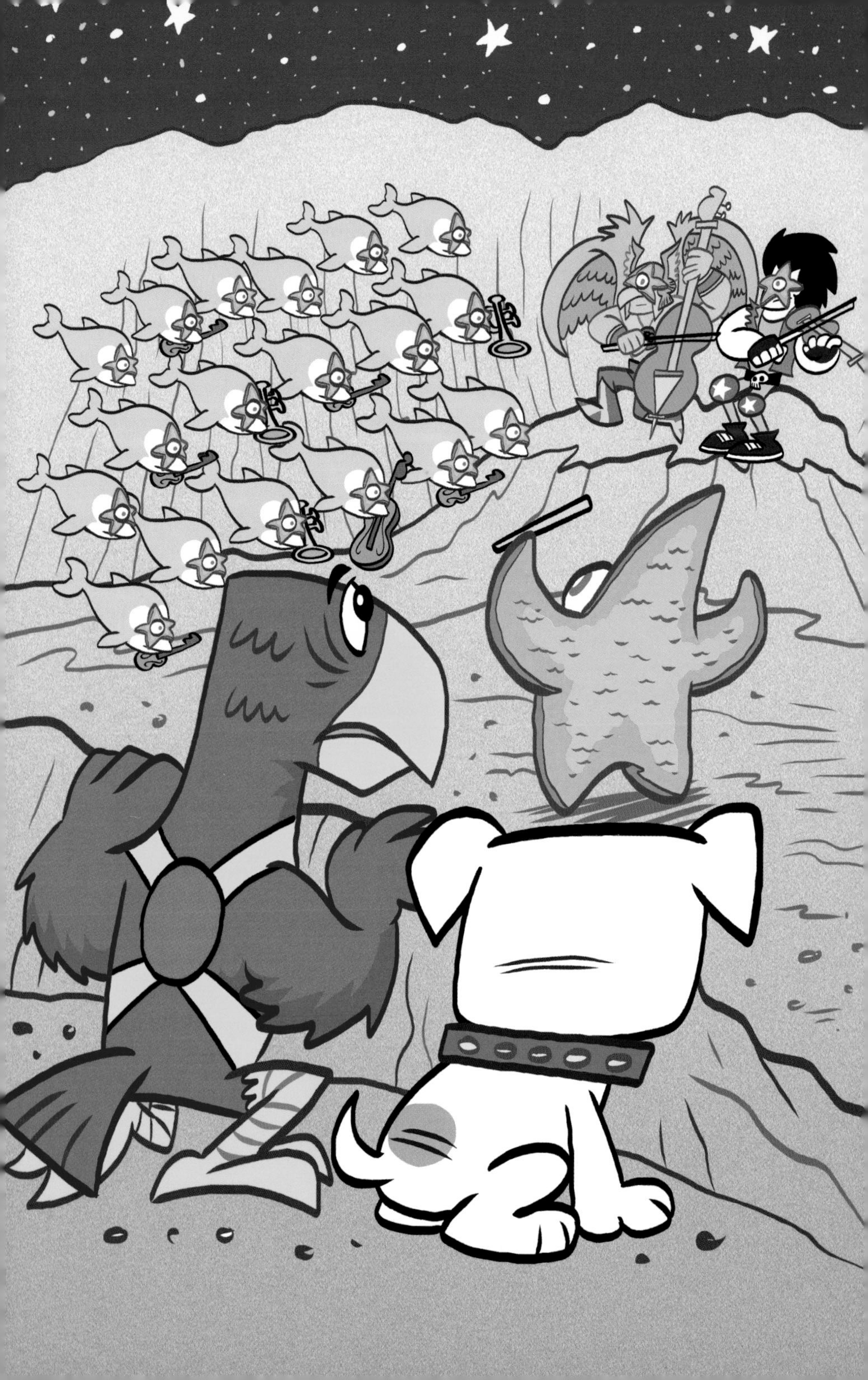

"**Dance! Dance! You magnificent Dolphins!**" shouted the giant Starro. "The most talented creatures in all the universe, and they are **MINE!**"

"I didn't know Hawkman could play the cello!" Big Ted exclaimed.

"Woof!!" barked Dawg with surprise.

"Lobo's doing very well on the violin, too," Big Ted added.

Suddenly, the giant Starro stopped conducting. "Who dares interrupt my concert?" he shouted from the stage.

"Uh-oh. He heard us!" said Big Ted.

**"Who dares to break my concentration?"** the giant Starro bellowed. The alien turned and spotted the Super-Pets. He stared at them with his one huge eye.

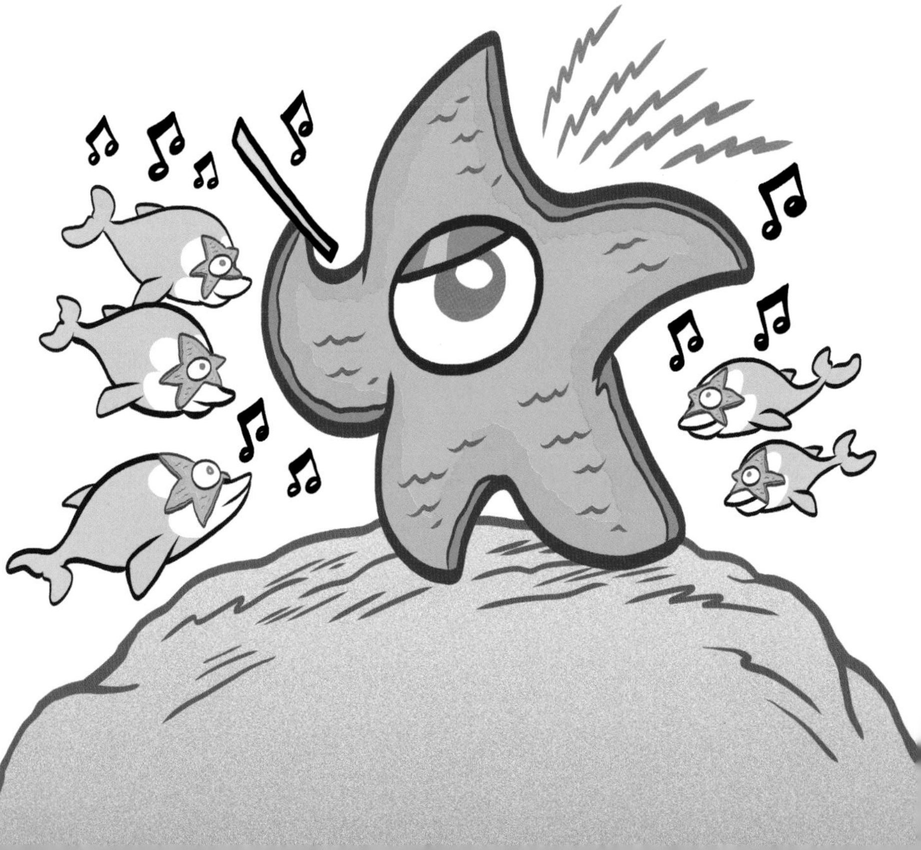

"OH! If it isn't the pet partners of my captive musicians," said the giant Starro. "What is the meaning of this downright rude interruption?"

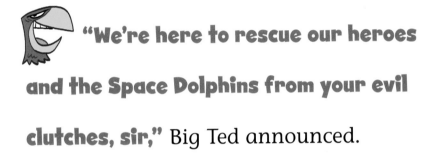 **"We're here to rescue our heroes and the Space Dolphins from your evil clutches, sir,"** Big Ted announced.

"Evil clutches, eh? Is that what you think of me?" questioned Starro. "I'm not really a bad starfish, you know. Misunderstood maybe, but not bad. I am just one who appreciates fine music and pure dolphin talent!"

"But why did you dolphin-nap these poor porpoises?" asked Big Ted. "Dawg misses them terribly!"

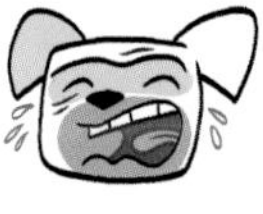

**WAHHH!! cried Dawg again.**

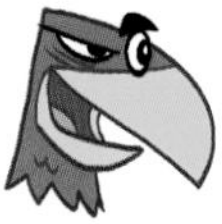

**"See?"** said Big Ted.

"I wanted the dolphins to perform for me and only me," said the giant Starro. "I have my own private space tank to keep them in. I'm tired of trying to buy tickets to their sold-out shows. If I can't see them perform, then no one can!"

Big Ted whispered to Dawg. "Oh man," he said, "that big Starro guy is really crazy."

**WOOF! Dawg agreed.**

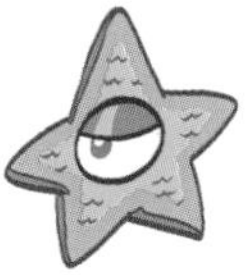

**"Not crazy! Just angry!"**

yelled Starro, overhearing the Super-Pets. "Now leave me alone so I can finish my concert!"

"Mr. Starro, sir?" asked Big Ted. "Could I suggest something?"

"What is it now?" said Starro, angrily.

 **"Your Starros are controlling the dolphins and telling them what to do, right?"** asked Big Ted.

"Yes. So?" questioned Starro.

"Maybe the talent isn't coming from the dolphins. Maybe it's coming from your very own minions," said Big Ted.

"What?" yelled Starro. "That's absurd!"

"How else would they know how to play music and dance?" asked Big Ted. "Let's try it, shall we?"

Suddenly, Big Ted grabbed a Starro and slapped it on Dawg's face. The mighty mutt began shaking and bouncing and dancing all over the concert stage. Dawg then grabbed the cello and the violin and the drums. He turned himself into a one-dog band!

"**WOW! You're right!** That dog has talent! Um, I mean, that Starro on his face has talent!" said the happy alien.

Moments later, the Super-Pets, the Space Dolphins, and all the Starros gathered on the crusty surface of the Starro Moon.

"You were right, Super-Pets," said the giant Starro. "My minions had the talent all along! You can have your Space Dolphins back. From now on, we're going to have our own concerts right here on our moon. Who knows, maybe *our* shows will be sold out too!"

"Thank you, Starro, for repairing our ship," said Hawkman, still wiping sticky Starro slime off his face.

"It was the least we could do, Hawkman!" answered Starro. "Happy trails, super heroes!"

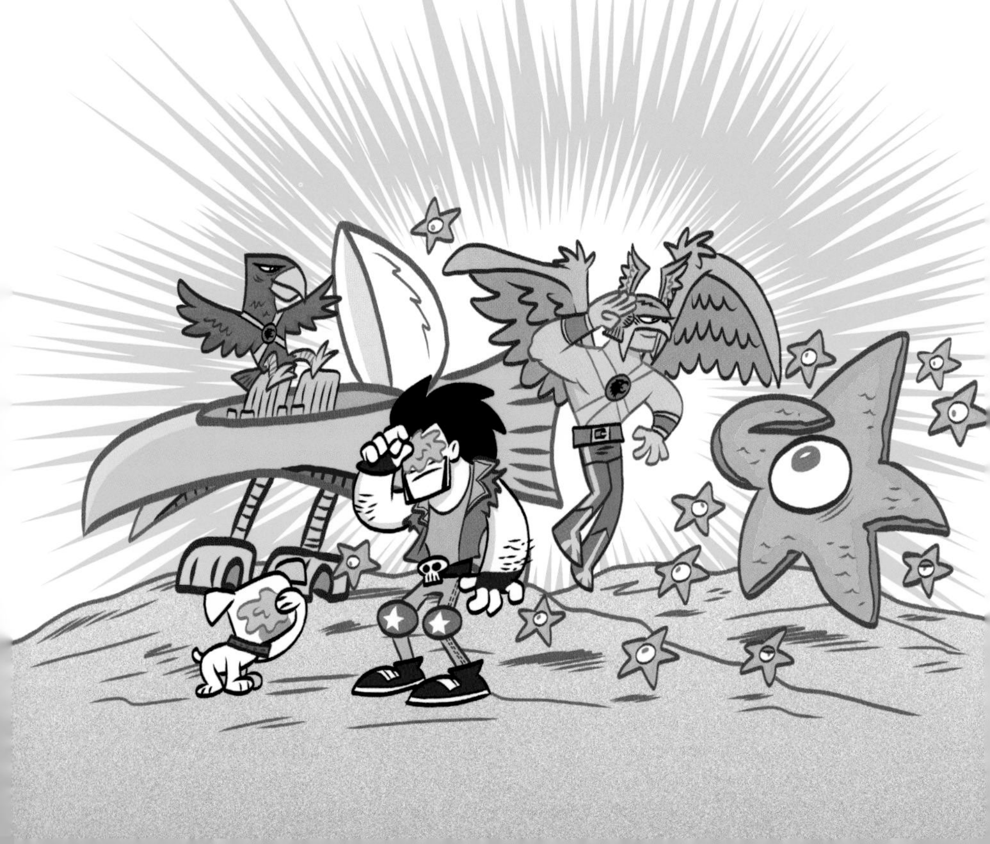

Hawkman, Lobo, Big Ted, and Dawg climbed aboard the spaceship. Big Ted pressed a few buttons. Then the group blasted off into space!

The Super-Pets said goodbye to the Space Dolphins and watched as the creatures swam off through the stars.

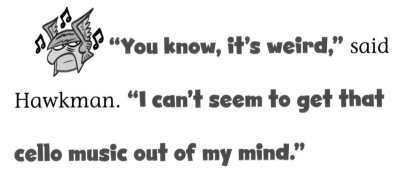 **"You know, it's weird,"** said Hawkman. **"I can't seem to get that cello music out of my mind."**

"I hear it, too," said Lobo. "Where can it be coming from?"

With puzzled looks, the heroes

turned around together and stared

toward the back of the ship. Dawg was

dancing and playing the cello with a

Starro still attached to his face.

"Well, the music is kind of nice,"

said Hawkman. **"You were right, Big**

**Ted, those Starros do have some**

**talent!"**

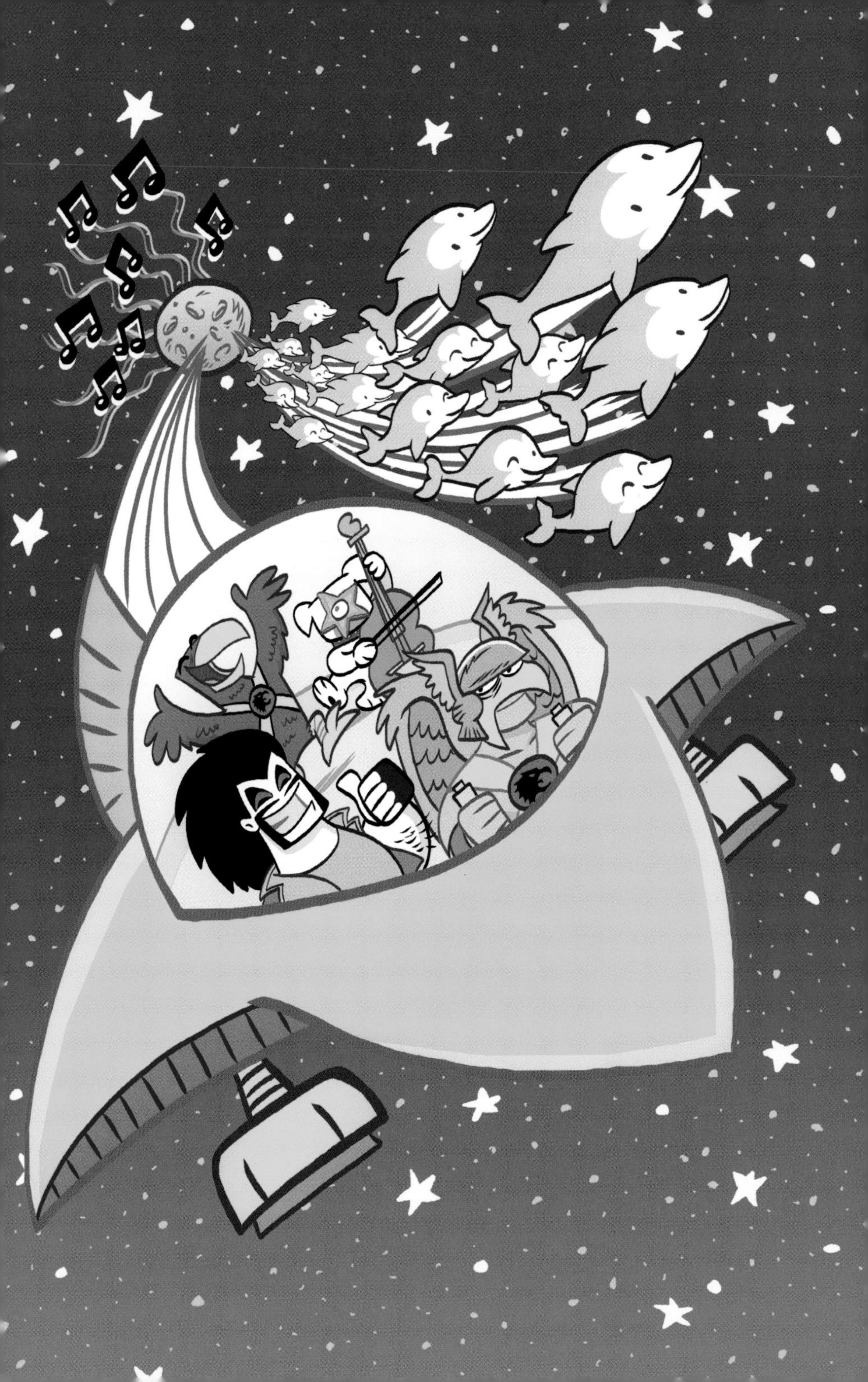

# KNOW YOUR HERO PETS!

1. Krypto
2. Streaky
3. Beppo
4. Comet
5. Super-Turtle
6. Fuzzy
7. Ace
8. Robin Robin
9. Batcow
10. Jumpa
11. Whatzit
12. Hoppy
13. Storm
14. Topo
15. Ark
16. Fluffy
17. Proty
18. Gleek
19. Big Ted
20. Dawg
21. Paw Pooch
22. Bull Dog
23. Chameleon Collie
24. Hot Dog
25. Tail Terrier
26. Tusky Husky
27. Mammoth Mutt
28. Rex the Wonder Dog
29. B'dg
30. Sen-Tag
31. Fendor
32. Stripezoid
33. Zallion
34. Ribitz
35. Bzzd
36. Gratch
37. Buzzoo
38. Fossfur
39. Zhoomp
40. Eeny

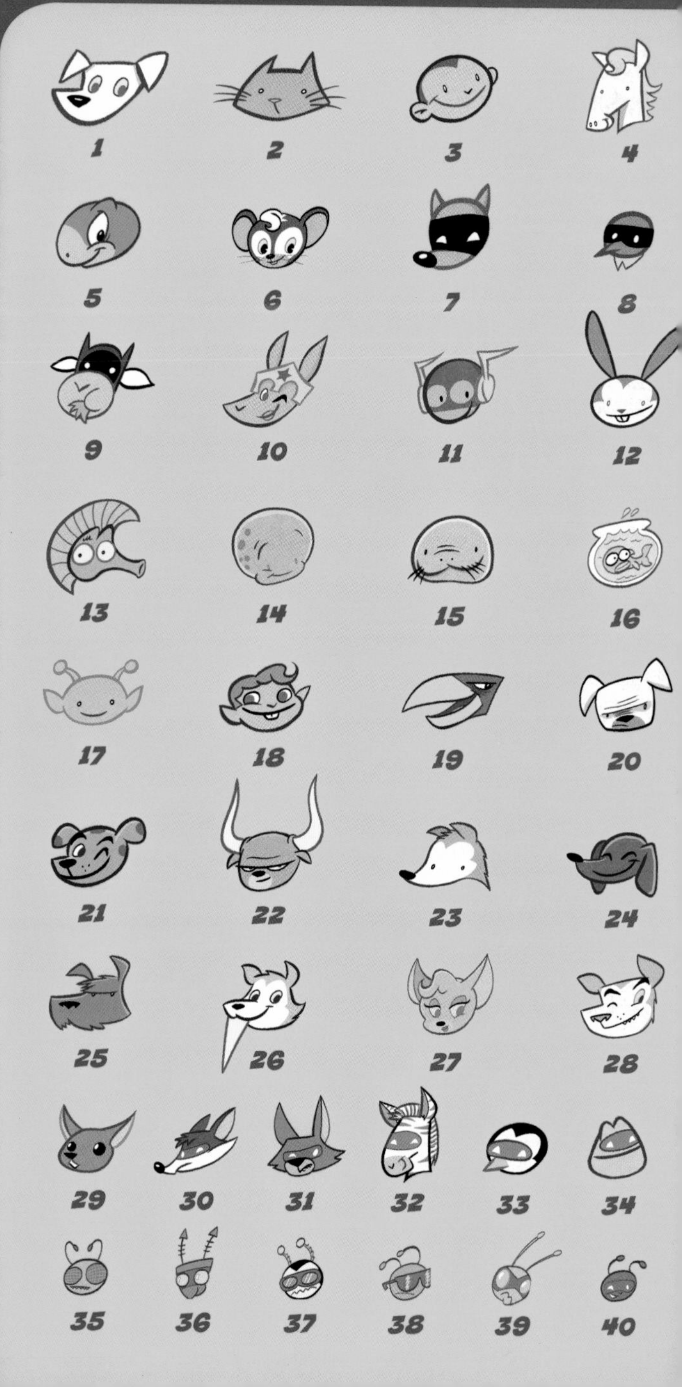
1
2
3
4
5
6
7
8
9
10
11
12
13
14
15
16
17
18
19
20
21
22
23
24
25
26
27
28
29
30
31
32
33
34
35
36
37
38
39
40

# KNOW YOUR VILLAIN PETS!

1. Bizarro Krypto
2. Ignatius
3. Brainicat
4. Mechanikat
5. Crackers
6. Giggles
7. Joker Fish
8. Rozz
9. Artie Puffin
10. Griff
11. Waddles
12. Mad Catter
13. Dogwood
14. Chauncey
15. Misty
16. Sneezers
17. General Manx
18. Nizz
19. Fer-El
20. Titano
21. Mr. Mind
22. Sobek
23. Bit-Bit
24. X-43
25. Starro
26. Dex-Starr
27. Glomulus
28. Rhinoldo
29. Whoosh
30. Pronto
31. Snorrt
32. Rolf
33. Squealer
34. Kajunn
35. Tootz
36. Eezix
37. Donald
38. Waxxee
39. Fimble
40. Webbik

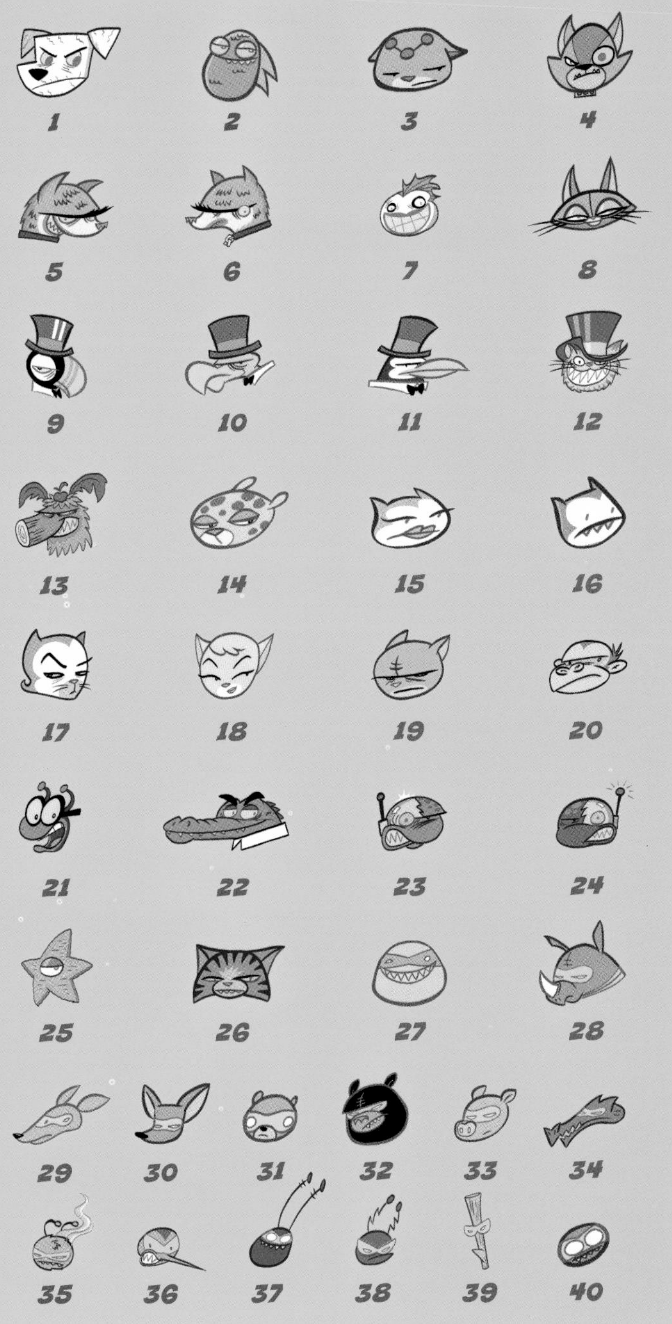

1
2
3
4
5
6
7
8
9
10
11
12
13
14
15
16
17
18
19
20
21
22
23
24
25
26
27
28
29
30
31
32
33
34
35
36
37
38
39
40

# MEET THE AUTHOR AND ILLUSTRATOR!

## Eisner Award-winner Art Baltazar

Art Baltazar is a cartoonist machine from the heart of Chicago! He defines cartoons and comics not only as an art style, but as a way of life. Currently, Art is the creative force behind *The New York Times* best-selling, Eisner Award-winning, DC Comics series Tiny Titans, and the co-writer for *Billy Batson and the Magic of SHAZAM!* Art is living the dream! He draws comics and never has to leave the house. He lives with his lovely wife, Rose, big boy Sonny, little boy Gordon, and little girl Audrey. Right on!

# WORD POWER!

**activated** (AK-tuh-vay-tuhd)—turned on something or caused it to work

**appreciate** (uh-PREE-shee-ate)—to enjoy or value somebody or something

**collision** (kuh-LIH-juhn)—two objects crashing together at high speeds

**distress** (diss-TRESS)—in need of help

**minion** (MIN-yuhn)—a follower who dutifully serves its master

**orchestra** (OR-kuh-struh)—a large group of musicians who play instruments together

**sidecar** (SYD-kar)—a car attached to the side of a motorcycle for a passenger

**sushi** (SOO-shee)—a Japanese dish made of raw fish or seafood pressed into rice

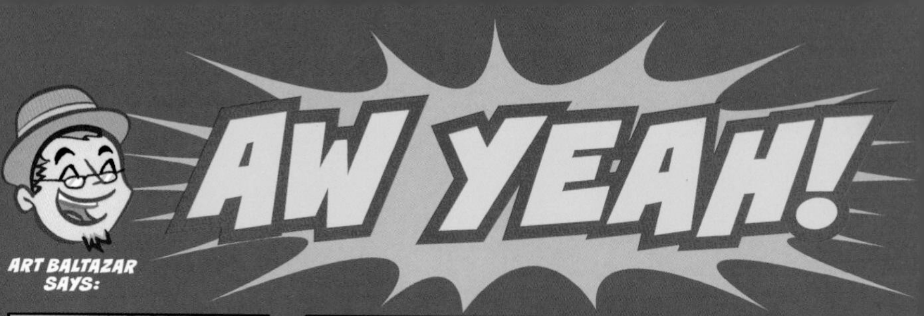
ART BALTAZAR SAYS:
AW YEAH!

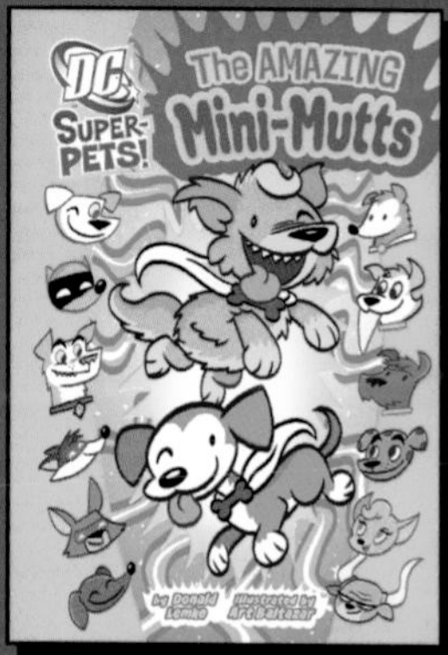
DC SUPER-PETS!
The AMAZING Mini-Mutts
by Donald Lemke
illustrated by Art Baltazar

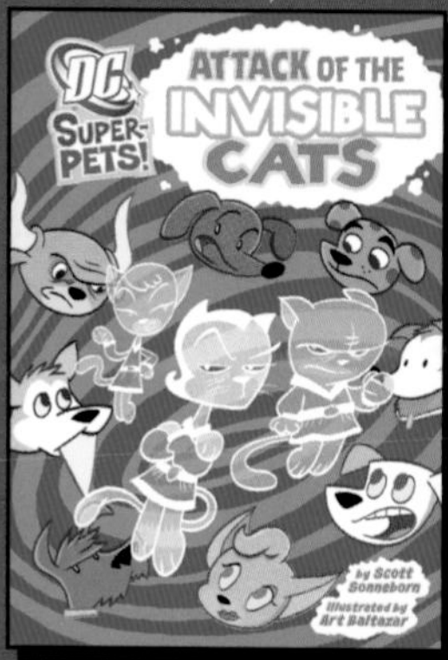
DC SUPER-PETS!
ATTACK OF THE INVISIBLE CATS
by Scott Sonneborn
illustrated by Art Baltazar

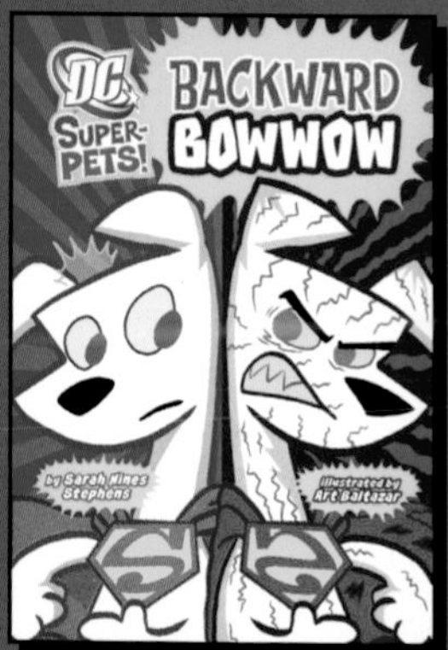
DC SUPER-PETS!
BACKWARD BOWWOW
by Sarah Hines Stephens
illustrated by Art Baltazar

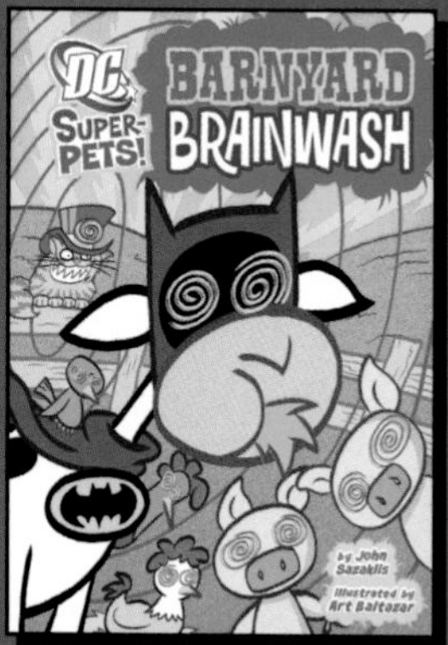
DC SUPER-PETS!
BARNYARD BRAINWASH
by John Sazaklis
illustrated by Art Baltazar

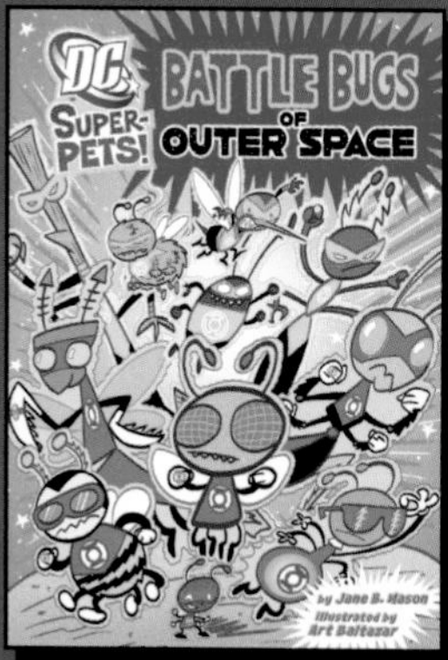
DC SUPER-PETS!
BATTLE BUGS OF OUTER SPACE
by Jane B. Mason
illustrated by Art Baltazar

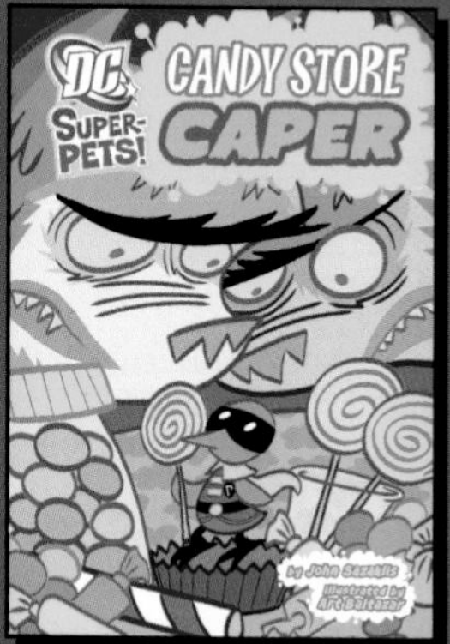
DC SUPER-PETS!
CANDY STORE CAPER
by John Sazaklis
illustrated by Art Baltazar

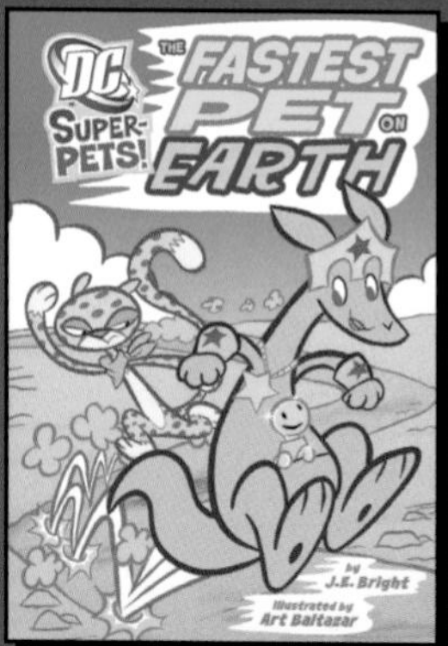
DC SUPER-PETS!
THE FASTEST PET ON EARTH
by J.E. Bright
illustrated by Art Baltazar

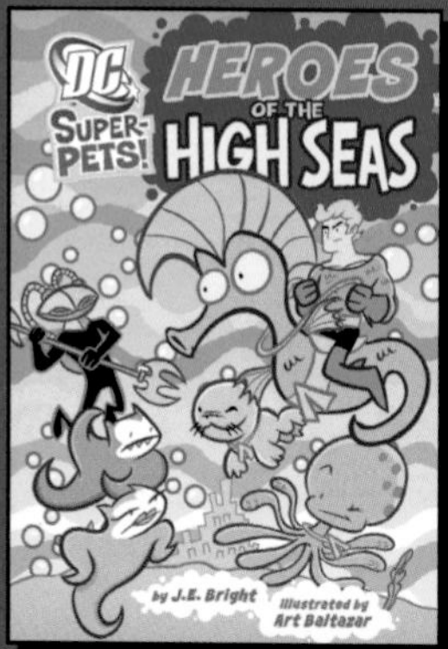
DC SUPER-PETS!
HEROES OF THE HIGH SEAS
by J.E. Bright
illustrated by Art Baltazar

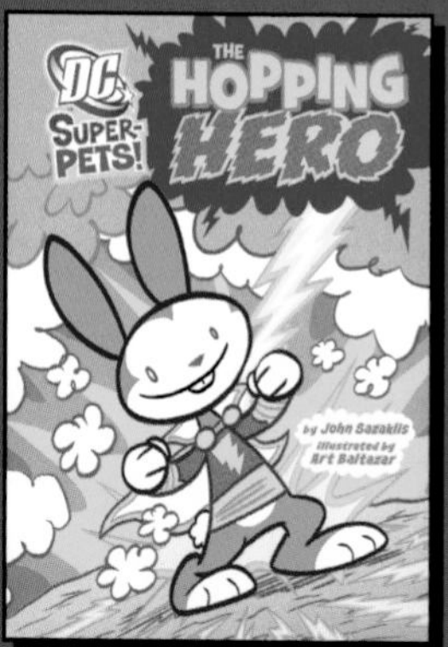
DC SUPER-PETS!
THE HOPPING HERO
by John Sazaklis
illustrated by Art Baltazar

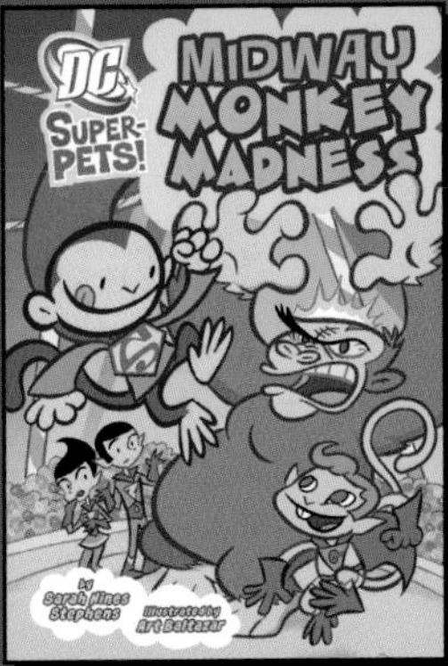
DC SUPER-PETS!
MIDWAY MONKEY MADNESS
by Sarah Hines Stephens
illustrated by Art Baltazar

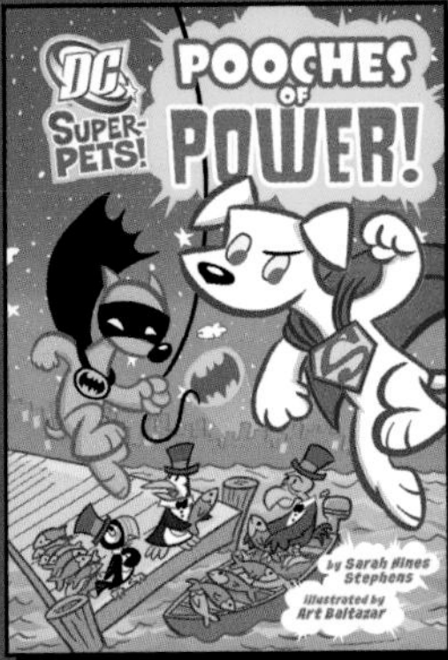
DC SUPER-PETS!
POOCHES OF POWER!
by Sarah Hines Stephens
illustrated by Art Baltazar

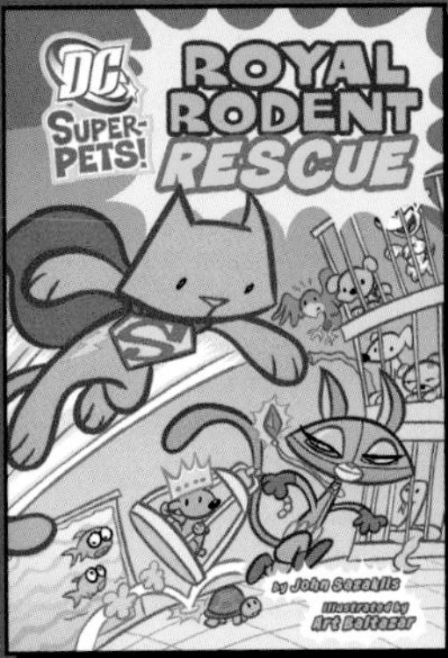
DC SUPER-PETS!
ROYAL RODENT RESCUE
by John Sazaklis
illustrated by Art Baltazar

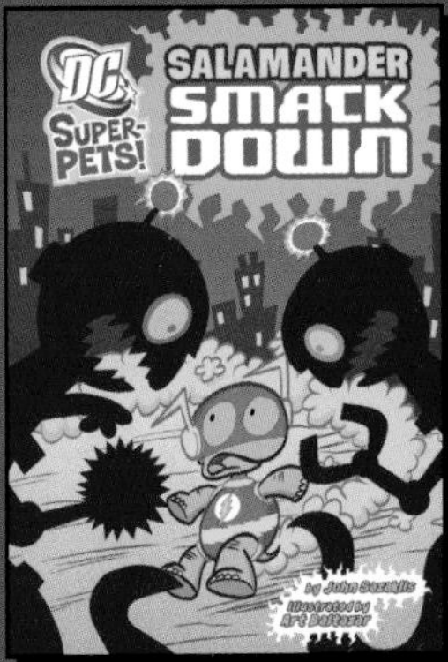
DC SUPER-PETS!
SALAMANDER SMACKDOWN
by John Sazaklis
illustrated by Art Baltazar

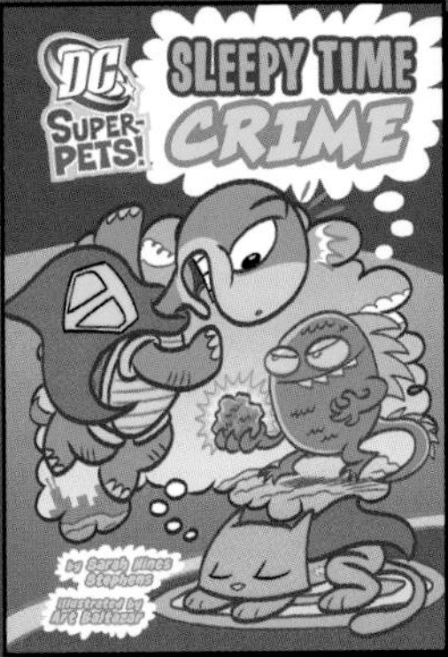
DC SUPER-PETS!
SLEEPY TIME CRIME
by Sarah Hines Stephens
illustrated by Art Baltazar

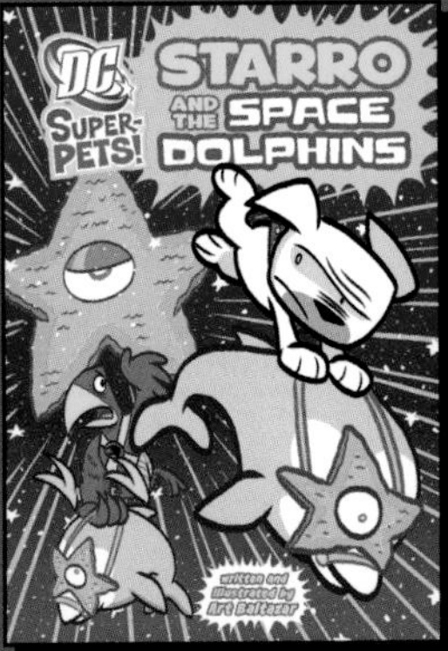
DC SUPER-PETS!
STARRO AND THE SPACE DOLPHINS
written and illustrated by Art Baltazar

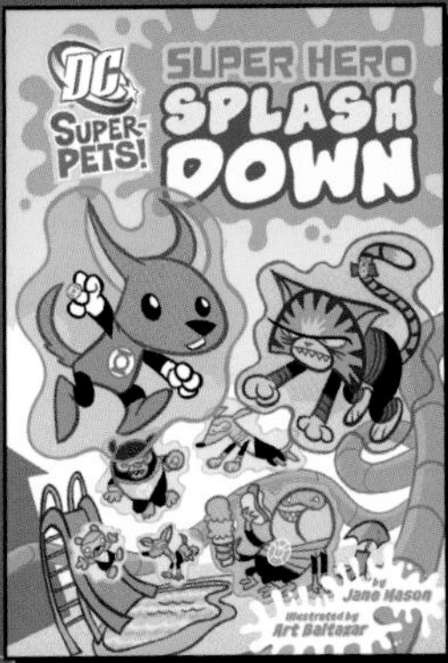
DC SUPER-PETS!
SUPER HERO SPLASHDOWN
by Jane Mason
illustrated by Art Baltazar

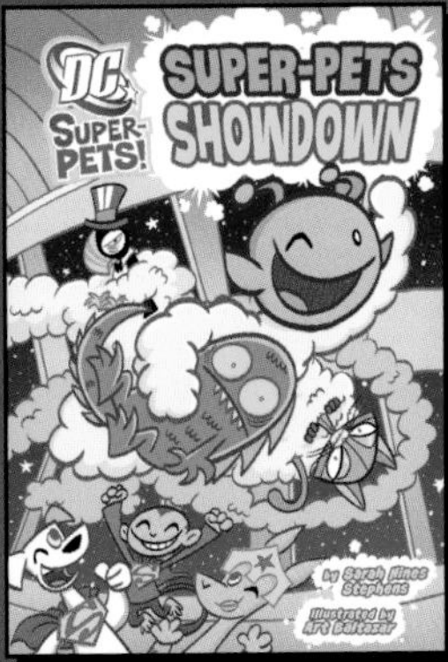
DC SUPER-PETS!
SUPER-PETS SHOWDOWN
by Sarah Hines Stephens
illustrated by Art Baltazar

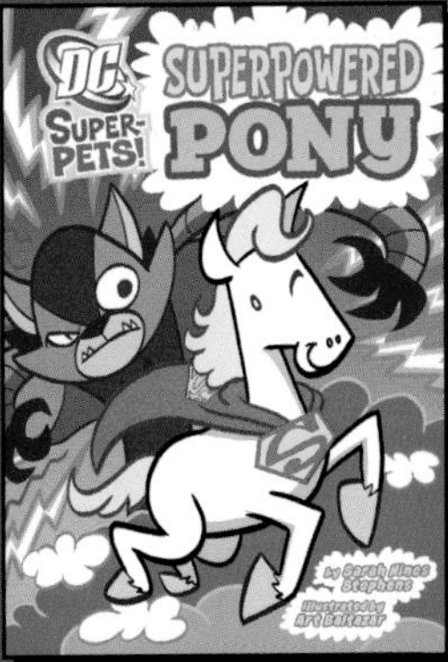
DC SUPER-PETS!
SUPERPOWERED PONY
by Sarah Hines Stephens
illustrated by Art Baltazar

**Read all of these totally awesome DC SUPER-PETS stories today!**

⊞ **Picture Window Books**™

Published in 2012
A Capstone Imprint
1710 Roe Crest Drive
North Mankato, MN 56003
www.capstonepub.com

Cataloging-in-Publication Data is available
at the Library of Congress website.
ISBN: 978-1-4048-6487-0 (library binding)
ISBN: 978-1-4048-7217-2 (paperback)

Summary: When Lobo's beloved Space
Dolphins go missing, Dawg and Big Ted
team up. Soon, they discover that the evil
Starros have attached themselves to the
poor porpoises and control them with their
powers. If the Super-Pets can't help, these
brainwashed bottlenoses will become a
whale of a problem!

Art Director & Designer: Bob Lentz
Editor: Donald Lemke
Creative Director: Heather Kindseth
Editorial Director: Michael Dahl

Printed in the United States of America
in Stevens Point, Wisconsin.
032012        006654R

DC™

SUPER-PETS!

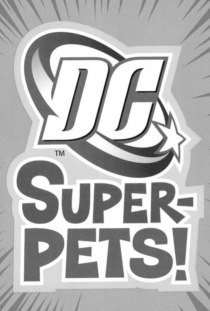

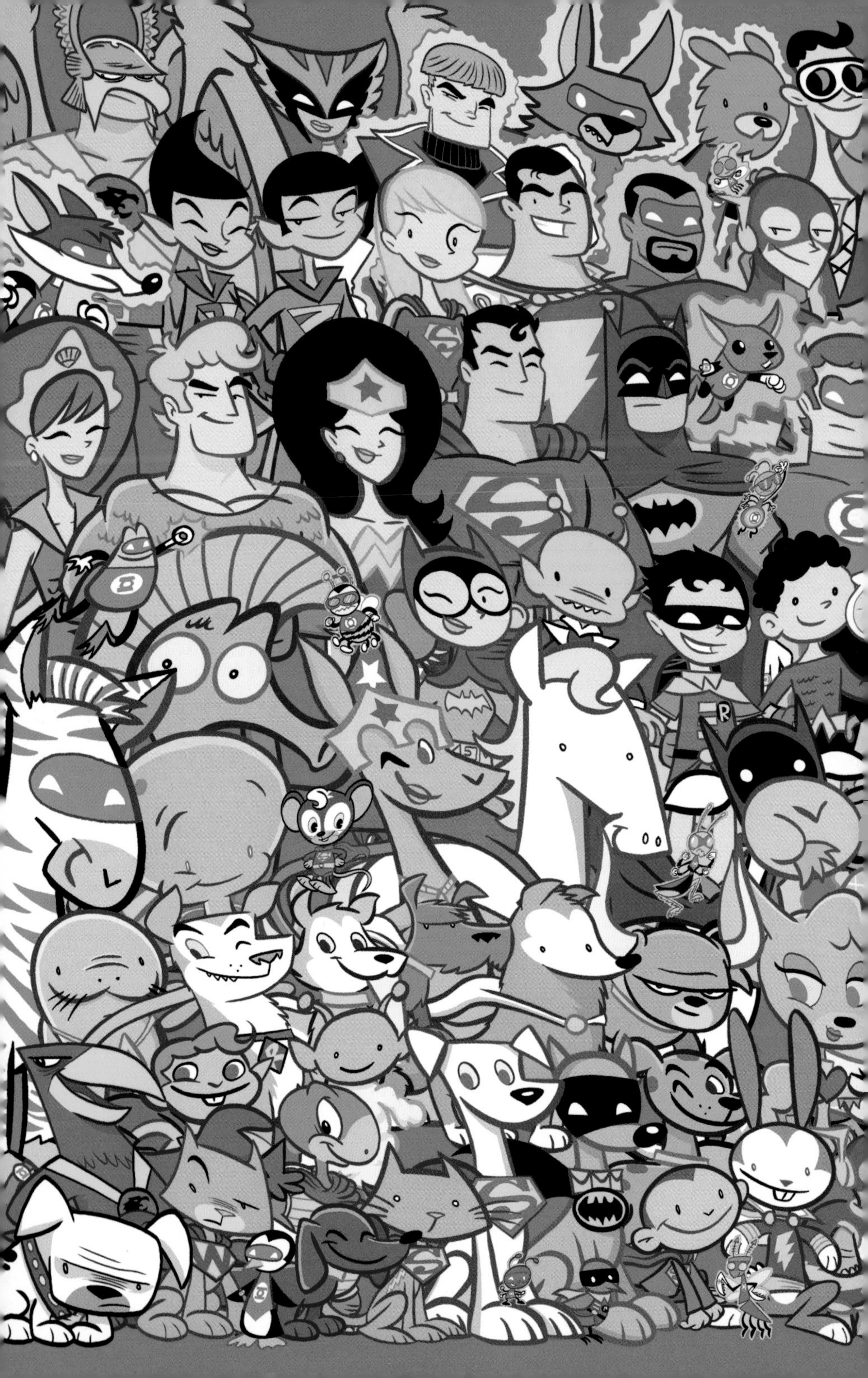

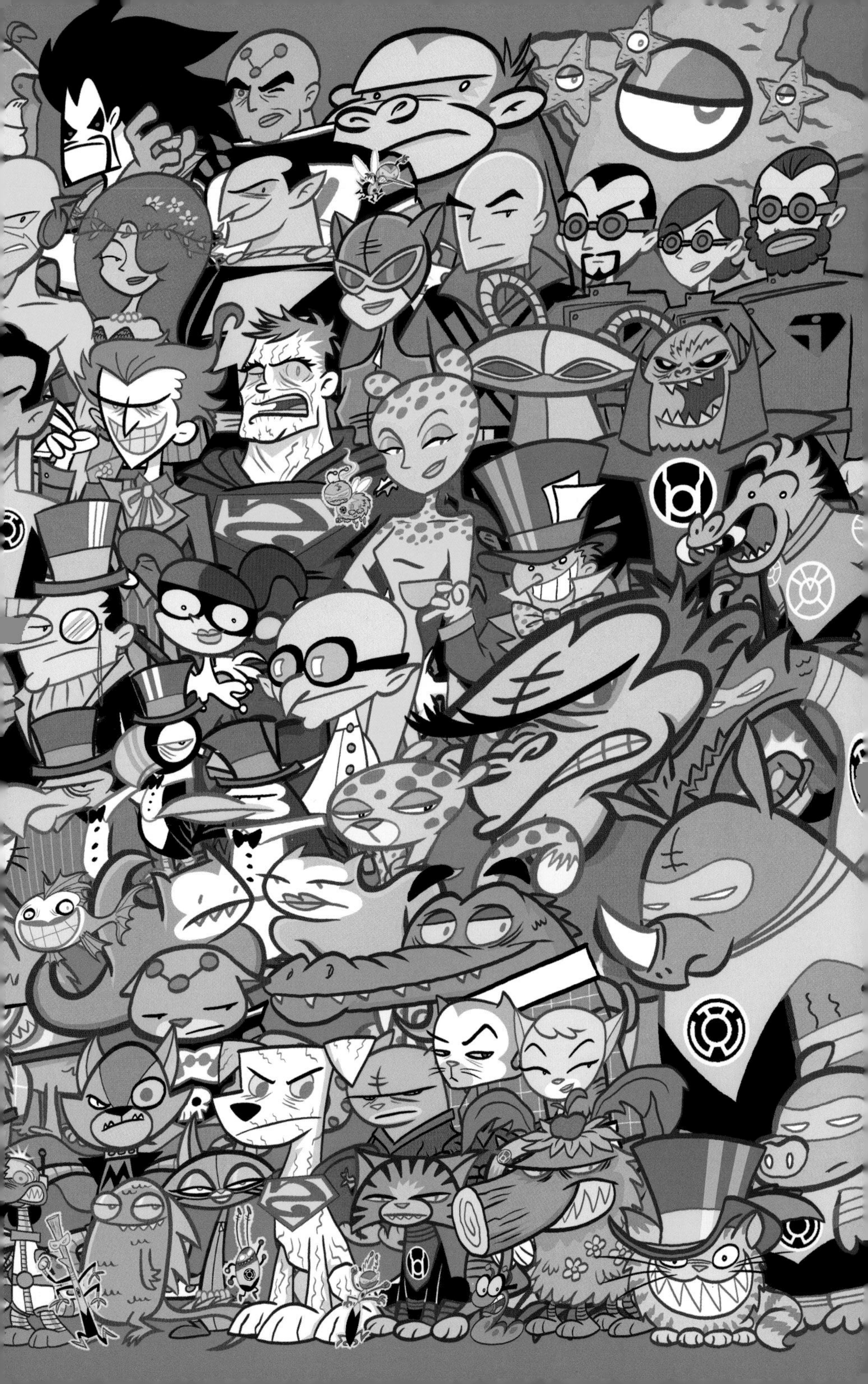

DC™

SUPER-PETS!

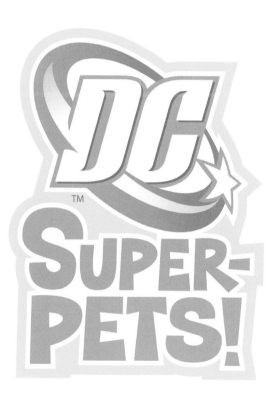